The Cotter's

First published 1982 by Abelard-Schuman Ltd.,

Copyright © Rod Campbell 1982
All rights reserved
First American edition 1983 by Four Winds Press

ISBN 0 590 07868 2

Published by Four Winds Press,
a division of Scholastic Inc., 730 Broadway, New York, NY 10003

Library of Congress Catalog Card Number 82-83224
Printed and bound in Singapore

Dear Zoo

Rod Campbell

Four Winds Press

New York

I wrote to the zoo

to send me a pet.

They sent me an...

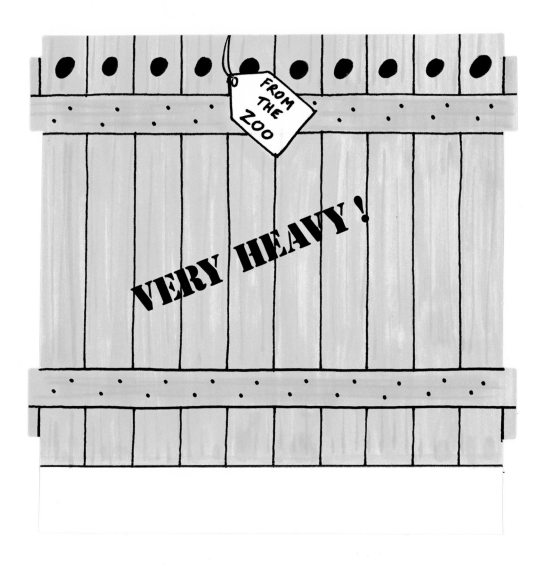

He was too big!
I sent him back.

So they sent me a...

He was too tall!
I sent him back.

So they sent me a ...

He was too fierce!
I sent him back.

So they sent me a ...

He was too grumpy!
I sent him back.

So they sent me a ...

He was too scary!
I sent him back.

So they sent me a ...

He was too naughty!
I sent him back.

So they sent me a ...

He was too jumpy!
I sent him back.

So they thought

very hard, and

sent me a ...

He was perfect!

I kept him.